MR.
CHATTERBOX

by Roger Hargreaves

D0522718

Mr Chatterbox was one of those people who simply couldn't stop talking.

He used to talk to anybody and everybody about anything and everything, going on and on and on.

And on and on and on!

And on and on and on!

And, when he didn't have anybody else to talk to, he used to talk to himself.

"Good morning, Mr Chatterbox," he used to say to himself.

"Good morning to you," he used to reply to himself.

"Nice day, isn't it?"

"Yes it is for the time of year."

And so on, and so on, and on and on!

He lived in a box shaped house in a village.

Chatterbox Cottage!

One morning the postman arrived with a letter for him.

"Morning Mr Chatterbox," said the postman.

"Ah, good morning to you, Postman," replied Mr Chatterbox. "Although, as I was saying to myself only yesterday, or was it the day before, I forget, however, it's not quite so good a morning, in my opinion, but I might be wrong, although I'm not very often, as it was the other day, Monday I think it was, or perhaps it was Tuesday, but never mind, because it is quite a good morning, don't you agree, yes of course you do, because that's what you said to me in the first place, and . . ."

And he went on and on, all morning, and the poor postman was late delivering all his letters.

That afternoon Mr Chatterbox went into the hat shop in the village.

"Hello, Mr Bowler," he said to the man who owned the hat shop. "Do you think, if it's possible, that I could buy, if it's not too expensive, but I'm sure it won't be, a new hat, because, would you believe it, yes of course you would, but anyway, as I was saying, my present hat, the one on my head, as you can see, is getting, how can I put it, a little too old, because I've had it for, let me see now, it must be, let's think, ten years, no, I tell a lie, it can't be that long, or can it, well yes it could be, but on the other hand . . ."

And he went on and on all afternoon and half the night, long after poor Mr Bowler should have shut up shop and gone home.

Eventually, when Mr Bowler managed to get a word in edgeways (or was it sideways), he promised to order a new hat for Mr Chatterbox.

Then he pushed Mr Chatterbox out of his shop, still talking of course, and went home for his supper, which was cold of course, because Mrs Bowler had cooked it for him hours ago.

And, while he ate, he thought.

Exactly one week later the new hat for Mr Chatterbox arrived, in a smart red hatbox.

The postman delivered it to Mr Bowler's shop.

"At last," said Mr Bowler, heaving a sigh of relief. "I think this hat is going to be the answer to the problem of Mr Chatterbox talking so much."

"I wish it could be," said the postman. "But how can it?"

"Because," replied Mr Bowler, "this hat is a magic hat!"

"Oh," replied the postman, who didn't quite understand.

That same afternoon Mr Bowler took the new hat round to Chatterbox Cottage.

"Oh, goody," said Mr Chatterbox, seizing the hatbox and opening it. "It's my new hat, my lovely new hat, I couldn't wait for it to arrive, in fact, I got up early this morning, because, aren't I silly, I just knew, I don't know how, but I really knew, you know, that today would be the day, I don't know how I knew, but I knew, and it is, and here's my hat, and oh, isn't it beautiful, I can't wait to try it on, oh I do hope it suits me, do you think it will, yes of course you do, and . . ."

"Why don't you try it on," said Mr Bowler, grinning.

"Try it on? Yes, of course I must try it on, how silly of me to stand here chattering on when I haven't tried it on yet, yes, I will, absolutely, definitely, try it on straight away, because, as I said, it's silly just to talk about trying it on, and then not try it on, isn't it, and so . . ."

He took the hat out of the hatbox, and put it on.

It was a beautiful hat!

"I say," he said. "I must say, yes I really must, that this hat, is, yes it really is, to say the least, one of the better hats that I have ever seen in my life, and in my life, I must say, I have seen some hats, and furthermore . . ."

But while he was talking a funny thing was happening.

The more words that came out of Mr Chatterbox's mouth, the larger his hat became.

The more Mr Chatterbox talked, the more the hat grew, and grew.

Mr Chatterbox kept on talking, and the hat kept on growing.

"I can't see anything," he said. "One minute I was standing here looking at my new hat in the mirror, and now, all of a sudden, without any warning, taking me all unawares, just like that . . ."

The hat grew down to his feet, and Mr Chatterbox stopped talking.

And, as soon as he stopped talking, the hat grew smaller and smaller, until it was the same size as when he'd first tried it on.

Mr Bowler had gone when Mr Chatterbox couldn't see him.

And now he was walking back to his shop. "My special magic hat really works," he chuckled.

The following day Mr Chatterbox was out for a walk when he met the postman in the village.

"Hello, Postman," he said. "I say, do you like my new hat, have you ever seen such a fine hat, I'm sure you never have, what a hat, and . . ."

But you know what was happening, don't you?

The hat grew and grew and grew the more Mr Chatterbox talked.

"Now I know what Mr Bowler meant by a magic hat," chuckled the postman.

And he went on his way, leaving poor Mr Chatterbox speechless.

"Hmm," he thought, thinking. Not talking – thinking!

And do you know something?

That hat taught Mr Chatterbox his lesson.

And these days he doesn't talk half as much as he used to, or even a quarter as much. And you know the reason for that, don't you?

Yes, of course you do.

But . . .

Keep it under your hat!

3 Great Offers for MR.MEN Fans!

MR.MEN TOKEN

1 New Mr. Men or Little Miss Library Bus Presentation Cases

A brand new stronger, roomier school bus library box, with sturdy carrying handle and stay-closed fasteners.
The full colour, wipe-clean boxes make a great home for your full collection.
They're just £5.99 inc P&P and free bookmark!

☐ MR. MEN ☐ LITTLE MISS (please tick and order overleaf)

2 Door Hangers and Posters

PLEASE STICK YOUR 50P COIN HERE

In every Mr. Men and Little Miss book like this one, you will find a special token. Collect 6 tokens and we will send you a brilliant Mr. Men or Little Miss poster and a Mr. Men or Little Miss double sided full colour bedroom door hanger of your choice. Simply tick your choice in the list and tape a 50p coin for your two items to this page.

Door Hangers (please tick)
☐ Mr. Nosey & Mr. Muddle
☐ Mr. Slow & Mr. Busy
☐ Mr. Messy & Mr. Quiet
☐ Mr. Perfect & Mr. Forgetful
☐ Little Miss Fun & Little Miss Late
☐ Little Miss Helpful & Little Miss Tidy
☐ Little Miss Busy & Little Miss Brainy
☐ Little Miss Star & Little Miss Fun

Posters (please tick)
☐ MR.MEN
☐ LITTLE MISS

3 Sixteen Beautiful Fridge Magnets – any 2 for £2.00!

inc.P&P

They're very special collector's items!
Simply tick your first and second* choices from the list below
of any 2 characters!

1st Choice

- [ ] Mr. Happy
- [ ] Mr. Lazy
- [ ] Mr. Topsy-Turvy
- [ ] Mr. Bounce
- [ ] Mr. Bump
- [ ] Mr. Small
- [ ] Mr. Snow
- [ ] Mr. Wrong

- [ ] Mr. Daydream
- [ ] Mr. Tickle
- [ ] Mr. Greedy
- [ ] Mr. Funny
- [ ] Little Miss Giggles
- [ ] Little Miss Splendid
- [ ] Little Miss Naughty
- [ ] Little Miss Sunshine

2nd Choice

- [ ] Mr. Happy
- [ ] Mr. Lazy
- [ ] Mr. Topsy-Turvy
- [ ] Mr. Bounce
- [ ] Mr. Bump
- [ ] Mr. Small
- [ ] Mr. Snow
- [ ] Mr. Wrong

- [ ] Mr. Daydream
- [ ] Mr. Tickle
- [ ] Mr. Greedy
- [ ] Mr. Funny
- [ ] Little Miss Giggles
- [ ] Little Miss Splendid
- [ ] Little Miss Naughty
- [ ] Little Miss Sunshine

*Only in case your first choice is out of stock.

--- TO BE COMPLETED BY AN ADULT ---

To apply for any of these great offers, ask an adult to complete the coupon below and send it with the appropriate payment and tokens, if needed, to MR. MEN OFFERS, PO BOX 7, MANCHESTER M19 2HD

- [ ] Please send ____ Mr. Men Library case(s) and/or____ Little Miss Library case(s) at £5.99 each inc P&P
- [ ] Please send a poster and door hanger as selected overleaf. I enclose six tokens plus a 50p coin for P&P
- [ ] Please send me ____ pair(s) of Mr. Men/Little Miss fridge magnets, as selected above at £2.00 inc P&P

Fan's Name _____

Address _____

_____ **Postcode** _____

Date of Birth _____

Name of Parent/Guardian _____

Total amount enclosed £ _____

- [ ] **I enclose a cheque/postal order payable to Egmont Books Limited**
- [ ] **Please charge my MasterCard/Visa/Amex/Switch or Delta account** (delete as appropriate)

Card Number

Expiry date ___/___ **Signature** _____

MR.MEN **LITTLE MISS**
Mr. Men and Little Miss™ & ©Mrs. Roger Hargreaves

CUT ALONG DOTTED LINE AND RETURN THIS WHOLE PAGE